U0010740

我能從
詩人，
變成一首詩

OSCAR
WILDE

王爾德──著　張家綺──譯
Oscar Wilde

目錄

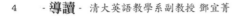

在一些線條的弧度裡，在某些色彩的美好與幽微中⋯⋯
——詩人藝術家王爾德

清大英語教學系副教授 鄧宜菁

　　王爾德不僅是個詩人，更常自詡為藝術家。他的生平和作品，都再再展現他對美與藝術的愛好，對美與藝術真諦的追尋。對他而言，「只有詩人是第一等的藝術家，因為他是色彩與形式的大師」。以此觀之，若果我們將王爾德稱為詩人藝術家，當非溢美之詞。

　　世人所熟知的王爾德是一名才華洋溢的劇作家。在《不可兒戲》、《溫夫人的扇子》等劇作中，他透過筆下的人物極盡嬉笑怒罵、嘲笑諷刺之能事。然而，除了劇作外，王爾德同時也創作詩歌、評論、童話與小說。他一生中所涉獵的文類堪稱廣泛。較少為人所注意的是，王爾德一直與藝術圈維持著緊密的關係，不僅十分關注當時藝壇的動靜與發展，也與不少藝術家有所往來，甚至交往密切，充分浸淫在其時代特有的文化氛圍中。從他早期的書信可以發現，此位愛爾蘭裔的英語文豪時常駐足於美術館與藝廊，觀看並冥思畫作。不論古典還是前衛的作品都能激發其想像力，源源不絕地供輸創作活動的能量。

　　在王爾德的時代，文學與繪畫相濡以沫，不僅相互啟發，更提供彼此重要的創作養分。王爾德在牛津求學時，對他影響甚鉅的兩位老師——華特・佩特（Walter Pater）與約翰・羅斯金（John Ruskin），皆兼具文學家與藝評家兩種身分。除了畫作之外，包括藝術理論、藝術思潮、藝術史，乃至於種種的藝術實踐，對形塑王爾德觀看的方式以及書寫的風格，影響皆不容小覷。由此看來，當我們閱讀其詩作時，若從繪畫的視角切入，或許會發現不少有趣的圖像元素。能言善道的王爾德不僅用文字傳遞了幽微的哲思與情感，更創造出華麗的印象與色彩。

王爾德在〈濟慈之墳〉[1]一詩中悼念並稱頌濟慈為「詩人畫家」。然而，其實在他自己的詩作中，王爾德也頻頻展露詩人畫家之姿。不僅憑藉景象來喻情，更透過語言符號來創造色彩、鑲嵌印象，猶如用文字在作畫。在他眾多色彩繽紛、充滿光影對照的詩作中，有一系列冠有「印象」一詞的作品，如〈清晨印象〉、〈印象：花園〉、〈印象：大海〉等。看到「印象」二字，有人可能會在腦海中閃過生活片段與畫面，但只要對藝術史略有涉獵的讀者，或許馬上就會聯想到十九世紀下半葉的印象派繪畫。在解析王爾德筆下的「印象」前，我們不妨先了解一下其語言與書寫特色。王爾德偏好借助慣用語詞來創造新義，從而顛覆原有意義。他尤其鍾愛挪用藝術思潮的流行語彙。王爾德選擇與使用語詞的方式往往導致他的語言表達呈現極富爭議性的多音與多義特性。印象一詞，在王爾德筆下，也因而常衍生出超越大眾認知的意義，會隨著情境變化，從而發展出諸多不同的意涵。印象既可以表述外在感官印象，亦可指涉內在印象，也就是王爾德反覆提及的「心境」（moods, états d'âme）。王爾德在他的作品中經常有意無意將「印象」與「心境」混淆使用。對他而言，不論是創作或評論，其目的皆在記錄自己的印象，而記錄的同時，也是在重溫及抒發自己的心境。印象也好，心境也好，主要都還是回歸、指向個人的情感，甚或激情。因而在閱讀他的「印象」詩作時，我們既可將其視為種種印象的抒發，也可解讀為詩人隱藏在語言、意象堆砌後的心境甚或情感。職是之故，我們不妨可將他的詩作（不論有無冠上印象一詞）看成詩人種種心情的剪影與印象。如〈聖米尼亞托〉、〈亞諾河畔〉及〈連葉〉等寫景、詠物之詩。在色彩運用及意象生成中，交織、突顯的是詩人凄涼、甚或絕望的心境。在塵世的寂寞中，景色的描繪似乎不再流洩出對崇高、浪漫的天真想望或寧靜冥想，而是對未知的世界，對看不見的彼岸，對死亡的想像與嚮往之情。

1　見《絕望的刀刺進了我的青春：王爾德詩選 I》。

身為一名作家，王爾德最早嘗試、且將其創作成果集結成書的文類，即是詩歌。然而，他的詩作卻是其作品中，一般讀者較少有機會接觸到的，或較容易忽略的類別。部分原因可能是受到批評傳統的影響。王爾德的《詩集》（Poems）雖是他第一部問世的作品，但自一八八一年出版後，就一直未得到評論者普遍的青睞。王爾德雖然曾在盛名時期加以修改並重新出版，但似乎並未徹底翻轉既定看法。在早期的詮釋模態中，缺乏原創性乃至於剽竊，是最常看到的負評。有評論者甚至聲稱在他的詩集中可偵測到六十來位詩人的聲音。然而，若將他的詩作置放於西方藝術發展的歷史與文化脈絡中來看，王爾德作品中的前衛特質以及其中暗藏的反思，可能就比較容易彰顯出來。

十九世紀下半葉，西方文明經歷巨變，人類生活的各個層面皆與昔日大不相同。種種前所未有、快速、大量的變革，刺激文學家、藝術家敏銳的心靈，並進而觸發他們創作上多樣的訴求。尤其越趨向世紀末，越可以從他們的作品感受到對待「世界」及「現實」的種種截然不同的態度，而這些不同的態度往往顯現並陳在同一時期生產的作品中，甚至在單一作品裡，都可以覺察到不同的聲音。在這一點上，王爾德的作品尤其具有代表性。古典、浪漫、寫實、印象、象徵的元素經常重疊或相互交織在同一作品中。其書寫中眾聲喧嘩的特質，甚至讓許多當代批評家將他視為後現代主義的先驅。

因而，當讀者仔細閱讀王爾德的詩作時，很難不察覺到，不論是字彙的選取、或者是意象的使用，常常顯現出多項重要文藝運動、思潮作用的軌跡，尤其是同時期印象派所開啟的繪畫革命。他的〈清晨印象〉的命名，巧妙地讓人聯想到印象派大師莫內一八七三年的著名畫作《印象：朝陽初昇》（Impression, soleillevant）。王爾德在〈謊言的式微〉（The Decay of Lying）一文中說道：「若不是有印象派畫家，我們怎麼會有那些絕妙棕色的雲朵，蟄伏在我們的街道，悄悄而行，迷濛我們的街燈，並讓兩旁的房子變化為驚悚的魅影呢？」如果換個切入的視角，從當時

倫敦藝文環境來看，王爾德這番話所指涉的，似乎就不僅是法國印象派畫家，更是與他亦友亦敵，在倫敦藝文界同樣別樹一格、極具爭議性的畫家詹姆斯‧惠斯勒（James Whistler）。

王爾德在創作初期，曾與此位大他二十歲的美國畫家來往甚密。惠斯勒的繪畫，在風格上迥異於當時強調主題及故事性的英國學院派畫作。他看重色彩在畫布上固有的張力與特質，極力創造色彩之間的對話，潛心探索繪畫的本質，因而常被視為印象派的先驅之一。為了突顯繪畫中用色、元素間的共鳴性，惠斯勒使用音樂術語來為他的畫作命名，期許色彩與筆觸如音符般完美和諧共奏。王爾德對惠斯勒作品中的「印象派」色調以及「聽覺」的特質，頗為驚豔，曾在評論中將惠斯勒的畫作與濟慈的詩相提並論，認為在兩者的創作中都可發現如出一轍的「音樂般的躍動」。對王爾德而言，惠斯勒作品中的顏色「交響曲」創造出獨一無二的圖像魅力。

值得一提的是，在印象派繪畫的孕生地——法國，坊間流通的印象派辭典將兩人皆收錄為重要索引[2]。回到王爾德的印象詩作來看，如同與惠斯勒唱合般，王爾德不僅在遣詞用字上，大玩顏色「交響曲」，在作品的命名上，如〈清晨印象〉、〈黃金屋：和聲〉及〈黃色交響曲〉等詩作，王爾德更是有意無意的回應惠斯勒畫作饒富音樂性的名稱。在〈清晨印象〉中，王爾德甚至還戲謔地重組了惠斯勒泰晤士河系列畫作的名稱。除了在作品上互相映照或互別苗頭，兩人間的美學論戰亦在十九世紀下半葉的藝術史及文學史喧騰一時。王爾德一八八二年在美國的巡迴演講曾受益於惠斯勒，同年年底，王爾德結束演講，啟程返回英國，旋即以藝術家之姿在倫敦社交界展露頭角。隔年，王爾德便受邀對皇家學院藝術學生演講，惠斯勒卻未獲邀請，其心裡的感受可想而知。或許更令惠斯勒不是滋味的地方在於，王爾德演講時似乎儼然將自己等同「藝術」的化身。此次事件埋下了兩人日後論戰的導火

2　如 Sophie Monneret, *L'impressionnisme et son époque*, tome I&II (Paris: Robert Laffont, 1980).

線。一八九一年，王爾德人在法國，惠斯勒仍難掩不平，寫信向詩人馬拉美（Stéphane Mallarmé）抱怨道：「（王爾德）無論到哪，閉口開口都是藝術，實在是汙染視聽，等著看罷，我們總有一天都會被他糟蹋的」。兩人的戰火於是一路延燒到英倫海峽的彼岸。要判定這場論戰誰輸誰贏，恐非易事。重要的是，在兩人言語激烈交鋒下，帶出了現代藝術的本質與價值的問題。

十九世紀末，在持續工業化、都市化、科技發明與地理發現、殖民拓展等劇烈變革的衝擊下，「藝術」的定義與疆界持續不斷受到挑戰。與時並進的王爾德自然不會自外於這股歷史洪流與藝文潮流。王爾德對藝術原創性的看法，尤其發人深省：

> 我所謂的原創性，亦即我們要求藝術家的，是處理上的原創性，而非主題上的。只有毫無想像力的人才執著於創新。真正的藝術家善於利用擷取到的素材，而且他什麼都不放過。

除了他的印象詩作，王爾德的情詩與含有宗教指涉的詩，似乎也巧妙印證著這樣的美學觀，並且隱隱呼應他在《格雷的畫像》中的著名警語，例如「愛情與藝術同樣是仿效」；「赦罪的並不是神，而是我們的懺悔」等。王爾德透過他的作品，不斷傳遞著特殊的美學觀乃至美學經驗，亦即：作品所折射出的並非只是人生，且絕非只是作者的人生，更是讀者自身。因而，個人色彩鮮明濃厚的唯美詩作，亦富含普世性的勸戒與啟示；而具濃重宗教色彩的詩作，詩人的懺悔與崇敬之情流動在五顏六色的印象與意象的堆砌和重組中，反倒弔詭地抽離了原有的宗教指涉與情境。語言符號既是告解的形式與工具，亦是終極目的所在。

王爾德，此位十九世紀晚期的文豪，以其特殊的書寫風格，與創作上涉足的多種文類，引起性質和程度不一的爭議與誤解，或褒或貶。面對不同的人生際遇，王爾德似乎隨時隨地採取一種藝術視角來觀察與省思浮生塵世。有一則關於他年輕時的軼事，

令人玩味之餘，亦頗能顯現他的態度與立場。他在牛津求學時，因喜好以美學家的姿態現身，被一群看不順眼的學校運動員拖到附近一處地勢較高的山丘上修理。王爾德並未積極反抗，只是在眾人一陣拳打腳踢之後，若無其事地起身，抖動身上塵土，望向遠方，說道：「從這山丘上看去的景色的確迷人。」

王爾德一生展現對藝術思潮、創作活動的高度敏感，不僅將所見所學轉化為書寫的動能與材料，更內化為一種生活態度與方式。對他而言，世界猶如一個絢麗多變的調色盤，而其中的正邪、好壞、生滅、垢淨，不過是組成花花世界的不同顏色或色調而已。此一獨到的眼光，讓他在詩作中不只覺察並刻畫出人世的興衰無常、矛盾荒誕，也讓他發現文字藝術重塑已知、進而探索未知的無限可能。

《格雷的畫像》中的畫家霍華，「在一些線條的弧度裡，在某些色彩的美好與幽微中」，瞧見了藝術的完美化身——格雷。閱讀王爾德的詩作時，我們不妨也隨著詩人暗藏的藝術家視角，透過文字所形構的圖像與線條，在光與影的縱橫交錯中，捕捉動人的意象與瑰麗的印象。

陌生人的淚水將為他填滿
那破碎已久、名為憐憫的甕,
只因哀悼他的人皆放逐者,
而放逐者永遠哀悼。

──王爾德墓誌銘,節自〈瑞丁監獄之歌〉

And alien tears will fill for him
Pity's long-broken urn,
For his mourner will be outcast men,
And outcasts always mourn.

──*The epitaph on Wilde's tomb, excerption from 'The Ballad of Reading Gaol'*

– San Miniato –

See, I have climbed the mountain side
Up to this holy house of God,
Where once that Angel-Painter trod
Who saw the heavens opened wide,

And throned upon the crescent moon
The Virginal white Queen of Grace,—
Mary! could I but see thy face
Death could not come at all too soon.

O crowned by God with thorns and pain!
Mother of Christ! O mystic wife!
My heart is weary of this life
And over-sad to sing again.

O crowned by God with love and flame!
O crowned by Christ the Holy One!
O listen ere the searching sun
Show to the world my sin and shame.

– 聖米尼亞托[1] –

瞧，我已經翻山越嶺
抵達上帝的神聖殿堂，
天使的畫家曾經造訪
望見敞開的天堂之門，

高坐在初升新月上弦，
慈悲聖母，純淨潔白——
瑪利亞！我願一睹您容顏
無奈死神遲遲不來。

噢，上帝以荊棘哀痛加冕！
基督之母！噢，神祕之妻！
我的生命令我力盡筋疲
再無法歌唱，肝腸寸斷。

噢，上帝以愛與烈焰封冠！
噢，獨一神聖的基督加冕！
噢，聽啊，仰望太陽前
請世界見證我的罪與恥。

---

1 義大利比薩省的市鎮，立於三座小山丘頂端，俯視亞諾河谷。

– By the Arno –

The oleander on the wall
Grows crimson in the dawning light,
Though the grey shadows of the night
Lie yet on Florence like a pall.

The dew is bright upon the hill,
And bright the blossoms overhead,
But ah! the grasshoppers have fled,
The little Attic song is still.

Only the leaves are gently stirred
By the soft breathing of the gale,
And in the almond-scented vale
The lonely nightingale is heard.

The day will make thee silent soon,
O nightingale sing on for love!
While yet upon the shadowy grove
Splinter the arrows of the moon.

Before across the silent lawn
In sea-green mist the morning steals,
And to love's frightened eyes reveals
The long white fingers of the dawn

– 亞諾河畔 [2] –

夾竹桃，倚牆靠，
黎明晨光裡，漸緋紅，
怎知黑夜暗影
籠罩翡冷翠，如棺罩。

露水閃爍山麓，
頭頂花兒爭妍鬥豔，
啊！蚱蜢已逃竄，
小小希臘之歌止息。

唯獨樹葉輕舞婆娑
隨著風兒溫柔一吐，
杏仁香幽幽的溪谷
猶聞夜鶯啼囀寂寞。

白晝終將要你噤聲，
繼續為愛唱，夜鶯！
然卻在幽影樹叢裡
月亮的箭碎成一地。

在跨越那凝止草地前
海綠色薄霧間清晨蟄伏，
在愛的驚恐雙眼前掀露
晨曦那根根修長白指。

2　義大利托斯卡尼地區的主要河流，流經翡冷翠（即今日的佛羅倫斯）和比薩。

疾速攀上東方天空
活逮扼殺顫慄的夜，
蠻不在意我心喜悅，
或夜鶯生命將告終。

Fast climbing up the eastern sky
To grasp and slay the shuddering night,
All careless of my heart's delight,
Or if the nightingale should die.

〈肉色和綠色的黎明：瓦爾帕萊索〉
（Crepuscule in Flesh Colour and Green: Valparaiso, 1866）

– Rome Unvisited –

I.
The corn has turned from grey to red,
Since first my spirit wandered forth
From the drear cities of the north,
And to Italia's mountains fled.

And here I set my face towards home,
For all my pilgrimage is done,
Although, methinks, yon blood-red sun
Marshals the way to Holy Rome.

O Blessed Lady, who dost hold
Upon the seven hills thy reign!
O Mother without blot or stain,
Crowned with bright crowns of triple gold!

O Roma, Roma, at thy feet
I lay this barren gift of song!
For, ah! the way is steep and long
That leads unto thy sacred street.

– 未訪羅馬³ –

I.

玉蜀黍的灰白轉紅，
我的心靈神遊前往
從清冷的北方城邦，
逃逸那義大利山嶺。

我的臉龐盼望著家，
當因朝聖之旅落幕，
但我暗忖，血紅烈日
將帶我前進神聖羅馬。

噢，萬福女王掌管
統領著你七座山麓！
噢，汙點瑕疵皆空的聖母，
頭戴光輝的三層黃金后冠！

噢，羅馬，羅馬，我擱在你腳邊
那首頌歌，多微不足道！
通往那神聖街道的路線
竟如此漫長陡峭。

3　王爾德在一八七五年夏天與友人遊歷歐洲，但盤纏散盡的他與朋友分別，獨自留在阿羅納，此
　詩是在紀念他無法探訪的羅馬。

II.
And yet what joy it were for me
To turn my feet unto the south,
And journeying towards the Tiber mouth
To kneel again at Fiesole!

And wandering through the tangled pines
That break the gold of Arno's stream,
To see the purple mist and gleam
Of morning on the Apennines.

By many a vineyard-hidden home,
Orchard, and olive-garden grey,
Till from the drear Campagna's way
The seven hills bear up the dome!

III.
A pilgrim from the northern seas—
What joy for me to seek alone
The wondrous Temple, and the throne
Of Him who holds the awful keys!

When, bright with purple and with gold,
Come priest and holy Cardinal,
And borne above the heads of all
The gentle Shepherd of the Fold.

II.
但踏出往南的腳步
前進台伯河口，
再度跪倒在菲耶索
我多心滿意足！

漫遊錯綜盤繞的松林
中止亞諾河的波光，
望見亞平寧山脈的黎明
奼紫薄霧和閃爍微光。

藏在葡萄園裡，數不盡的
灰色屋舍、果園和橄欖園，
直到從清冷的坎培納路徑
瞥見七座聳立天際的山脊！

III.
一介來自北方海洋的朝聖者——
形影單隻，尋找著美妙神廟
和擁有威震鑰匙的上帝王座
旅途是如此絕妙！

神父和那神聖樞機主教，
一身金粉霓裳，
凌駕萬眾之上
起伏山谷的溫馴牧羊人。

O joy to see before I die
The only God-anointed King,
And hear the silver trumpets ring
A triumph as He passes by!

Or at the altar of the shrine
Holds high the mystic sacrifice,
And shows a God to human eyes
Beneath the veil of bread and wine.

IV.
For lo, what changes time can bring!
The cycles of revolving years
May free my heart from all its fears,—
And teach my lips a song to sing.

Before yon field of trembling gold
Is garnered into dusty sheaves,
Or ere the autumn's scarlet leaves
Flutter as birds adown the wold,

I may have run the glorious race,
And caught the torch while yet aflame,
And called upon the holy name
Of Him who now doth hide His face.

Arona

噢，能在我有生之年
目睹上帝塗抹聖膏的唯一騎士，
聽見吹響的銀亮號角
宣告勝利降臨，而祂行經身邊！

抑或在神殿祭壇裡
神祕祭品高高舉起，
在麵包和葡萄酒的布塊下
掀露上帝，盡收眾人眼底。

IV.
哀哉，瞧那光陰變遷！
循環的歲月動盪
卸除我心底恐懼驚惶，——
教導我的唇吟唱。

遠方田野金黃輕顫
趁轉為粉色光束前，
或樹葉嫣紅的秋季降臨前
鳥兒振翅，低空飛向荒原，

我曾參與輝煌競賽，
接過熠熠輝耀火炬，
呼喊著祂神聖的名
而今祂卻掩著面容。

阿羅納

– La Bella Donna Della Mia Mente –

My limbs are wasted with a flame,
My feet are sore with travelling,
For calling on my Lady's name
My lips have now forgot to sing.

O Linnet in the wild-rose brake
Strain for my Love thy melody,
O Lark sing louder for love's sake,
My gentle Lady passeth by.

She is too fair for any man
To see or hold his heart's delight,
Fairer than Queen or courtezan
Or moon-lit water in the night.

Her hair is bound with myrtle leaves,
(Green leaves upon her golden hair!)
Green grasses through the yellow sheaves
Of autumn corn are not more fair.

Her little lips, more made to kiss
Than to cry bitterly for pain,
Are tremulous as brook-water is,
Or roses after evening rain.

– 我腦海中的美人 –

熊熊烈焰倦怠了我的四肢，
長途跋涉疼痛了我的雙腳，
聲聲呼喚著我愛人的名字
我的唇，竟忘了應該歌唱。

躲藏野薔薇裡的紅雀，
為了我的愛，升騰你的旋律，
為愛高聲哼唱的雲雀，
我溫潤如玉的愛人走了過去。

她的美，哪個男人夠資格
忘情凝視，抑或盡情擁有，
沒有皇后或交際名媛可及，
月光映照夜湖亦不可相比。

桃金孃葉盤繞著她的髮，
（金髮與綠葉相映成趣！）
澄黃髮絲透出綠草青青
秋日穀粒亦是相形見絀。

她的櫻桃小嘴，不為痛苦
哀號，是為親吻而生，
猶如溪水輕柔顫動，
抑或夜雨後的玫瑰。

Her neck is like white melilote
Flushing for pleasure of the sun,
The throbbing of the linnet's throat
Is not so sweet to look upon.

As a pomegranate, cut in twain,
White-seeded, is her crimson mouth,
Her cheeks are as the fading stain
Where the peach reddens to the south.

O twining hands! O delicate
White body made for love and pain!
O House of love! O desolate
Pale flower beaten by the rain!

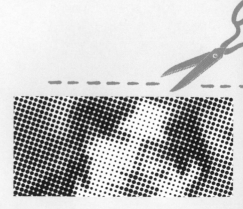

她猶如草木犀的雪頸，
因為驕陽的愉悅赧紅，
紅雀歌喉的輕顫
都不若她的嬌豔。

彷彿剖半番石榴的白籽，
呼之欲出她的豔紅唇畔，
她的豐頰猶如蜜桃暈紅
透出那漸漸褪去的色澤。

噢，她雙手的對稱！
噢，為愛與痛而生的雪白細緻身軀！
噢，裝載愛的樓舍！
噢，是飽經風雨，荒蕪蒼白的花朵！

〈白色交響曲第一號：白衣女子〉（Symphony in White, No.1: The White Girl, 1862）
畫中女子為喬安娜·希芬南（Joanna Hiffernan），是惠斯勒的模特兒與情婦。

〈喬〉（Jo, 1861）
喬安娜的素描肖像。

– Chanson –

A ring of gold and a milk-white dove
Are goodly gifts for thee,
And a hempen rope for your own love
To hang upon a tree.

For you a House of Ivory
(Roses are white in the rose-bower)!
A narrow bed for me to lie
(White, O white, is the hemlock flower)!

Myrtle and jessamine for you
(O the red rose is fair to see)!
For me the cypress and the rue
(Fairest of all is rose-mary)!

For you three lovers of your hand
(Green grass where a man lies dead)!
For me three paces on the sand
(Plant lilies at my head)!

– 香頌 –

黃金戒指，乳白鴿子
當作贈予你的獻禮，
再交予你一條麻繩
好讓你把愛掛樹頂。

將一棟象牙屋獻給你
（玫瑰棚的玫瑰白皙）！
留一張窄床給自己躺
（鐵杉花是多麼明皙）！

把桃金孃和茉莉花獻給你
（噢，紅玫瑰明豔動人）！
再把柏樹和芸香留給自己 [4]
（最美的莫過於迷迭香）！

把你手裡的三個愛人獻給你
（一片死了男人的青草）！
再留了沙地上的三步給自己
（在我的頭頂栽植百合）！

4　古時候柏樹的用途是誌哀，芸香的英文（rue）則和悔恨同字；埃及古墓常見迷迭香，據聞可讓
　　生者安定，死者安息。

- Lotus Leaves -

I.
There is no peace beneath the moon,—
Ah! in those meadows is there peace
Where, girdled with a silver fleece,
As a bright shepherd, strays the moon?
Queen of the gardens of the sky,
Where stars like lilies, white and fair,
Shine through the mists of frosty air,
Oh, tarry, for the dawn is nigh!
Oh, tarry, for the envious day
Stretches long hands to catch thy feet.
Alas! but thou art overfleet,
Alas! I know thou wilt not stay.

II.
Eastward the dawn has broken red,
The circling mists and shadows flee;
Aurora rises from the sea,
And leaves the crocus-flowered bed.
Eastward the silver arrows fall,
Splintering the veil of holy night:
And a long wave of yellow light
Breaks silently on tower and hall.
And speeding wide across the wold
Wakes into flight some fluttering bird;
And all the chestnut tops are stirred,
And all the branches streaked with gold.

– 蓮葉 –

I.
月光底下不見安寧——
啊！草地可有平靜？
那有銀白羊毛纏繞，
牧羊人教月亮迷惘。
遙遙穹蒼花園皇后，
星辰彷若百合，潔白淨美，
在迷濛霧氣茫茫閃爍，
噢，別走，黎明將至！
噢，別走，妒嫉白晝
伸出長長手臂，緊捉我腳。
唉！你卻已飛掠而過，
唉！我知你將不久留。

II.
東方天際，晨曦破紅，
迷霧黑影一溜煙飛逝；
曙光自海洋冉冉高升，
徒留下一片番紅花床。
東方天際，銀箭殞落，
劃破聖潔黑夜帷幕：
蛋黃色澤光波悠長，
寂靜墜落高塔廳堂，
匆匆掃過遼闊荒原
寐鳥驚動，振翅飛散；
七葉樹梢沙沙騷動，
枝頭灑滿金黃光芒。

III.

To outer senses there is peace,
A dream-like peace on either hand,
Deep silence in the shadowy land,
Deep silence where the shadows cease,
Save for a cry that echoes shrill
From some lone bird disconsolate;
A curlew calling to its mate;
The answer from the distant hill.
And, herald of my love to Him
Who, waiting for the dawn, doth lie,
The orbed maiden leaves the sky,
And the white firs grow more dim.

IV.

Up sprang the sun to run his race,
The breeze blew fair on meadow and lea,
But in the west I seemed to see
The likeness of a human face.
A linnet on the hawthorn spray
Sang of the glories of the spring,
And made the flow'ring copses ring
With gladness for the new-born day.
A lark from out the grass I trod
Flew wildly, and was lost to view
In the great seamless veil of blue
That hangs before the face of God.
The willow whispered overhead
That death is but a newer life
And that with idle words of strife

III.
表面依稀可感平靜，
兩手托著似夢靜謐，
斜影土地的寧寂，
黑影消逝的沉寂，
唯獨驚叫蕩漾的呼喊
來自悲不自勝的孤鳥；
是呼朋引伴的麻鷸；
遙遠山頭傳來回音。
使者傳遞我對祂的愛，
祂靜待著破曉天明，
飽滿少女揮別穹蒼，
雪白冷杉愈發幽暗。

IV.
晨陽東升，繞軌奔走，
微風徐徐，吹拂著綠地牧草，
我卻似在西方，瞥見
一張恍若人形的容貌。
紅雀在山楂樹枝鳴囀
歌頌春日的榮景美好，
開花結果的矮林間音符迴盪
為了這新生的一日歡喜歌唱。
我踩踏行走在草地
一隻雲雀熱烈飛舞
不著痕跡，無影遁入
披掛上帝面前的湛藍面紗。
頭頂的垂柳細語喃喃
死亡開啟了嶄新生命
悲慟言語不具意義

We bring dishonour on the dead.
I took a branch from off the tree,
And hawthorn branches drenched with dew,
I bound them with a sprig of yew,
And made a garland fair to see.
I laid the flowers where He lies
(Warm leaves and flowers on the stones):
What joy I had to sit alone
Till evening broke on tired eyes:
Till all the shifting clouds had spun
A robe of gold for God to wear
And into seas of purple air
Sank the bright galley of the sun.

V.
Shall I be gladdened for the day,
And let my inner heart be stirred
By murmuring tree or song of bird,
And sorrow at the wild winds' play?
Not so, such idle dreams belong
To souls of lesser depth than mine;
I feel that I am half divine;
I that I am great and strong.
I know that every forest tree
By labour rises from the root
I know that none shall gather fruit
By sailing on the barren sea.

只為死者帶來不敬。
我從樹梢摘下根枝椏，
露水浸濕了山楂枝椏，
再拿紫杉枝纏繞山楂，
編織美麗可人的花環。
將花兒擱放祂歇息地，
（溫暖枝葉花朵歇在石碑）：
我獨自坐在這兒多快活
直到夜晚籠罩疲憊雙眼：
直到變化萬千風雲繾綣
織出上帝身穿那副金袍
而萬丈光輝的落日帆船
將沉入萬千紫氣的海洋。

V.

我是否該為這日歡騰，
沙沙樹聲，吱喁鳥語，
牽動內心的騷動不安，
是否為狂風大作傷懷？
不，如此空乏的夢境
屬靈魂不具深度之人；
我感覺頗具神聖；
既強壯而且偉大。
我知每一株林木
含辛茹苦，拔地而生
我明瞭貧瘠大海航行
終將無人可收穫果實。

〈灰與銀：老貝特西河〉
（Grey and Silver: Old Battersea Reach, 1863）

－ 航海印象 －

海水是藍寶石的湛藍，而天空
亦如同蛋白石，在天空裡灼燒；
我們揚起船帆；吹拂和煦海風
啟程前往矗立東邊的蔚藍國度。
我的目光自陡峭船首匆匆掃視
扎金索斯島上的橄欖園和小溪，
伊薩卡島懸崖，李卡翁的雪峰，
還有那阿卡迪[5]山丘的花團錦簇。

船帆一陣陣拍打著桅杆，
船側激出海水波波漣漪，
船首傳出女孩笑聲，亦如漣漪，
是唯一聲音：——當西邊開始燃燒，
豔紅落日馳騁海平面，
我終於佇立希臘國土！

－ Impression de Voyage －

The sea was sapphire coloured, and the sky
Burned like a heated opal through the air;
We hoisted sail; the wind was blowing fair
For the blue lands that to the eastward lie.

5　位於希臘伯羅奔尼撒半島東部的區域，在希臘神話中，阿卡迪是潘神的家；歐洲文藝復興藝術裡，
　　阿卡迪則經常是人間淨土的代名詞。

From the steep prow I marked with quickening eye
Zakynthos, every olive grove and creek,
Ithaca's cliff, Lycaon's snowy peak,
And all the flower-strewn hills of Arcady.

The flapping of the sail against the mast,
The ripple of the water on the side,
The ripple of girls' laughter at the stern,
The only sounds: —when 'gan the West to burn,
And a red sun upon the seas to ride,
I stood upon the soil of Greece at last!

〈肉色與紅的和聲〉（Harmony in Flesh Colour and Red, 1869）

– Urbs Sacra Æterna –

Rome! what a scroll of History thine has been
In the first days thy sword republican
Ruled the whole world for many an age's span:
Then of thy peoples thou wert crownèd Queen,
Till in thy streets the bearded Goth was seen;
And now upon thy walls the breezes fan
(Ah, city crowned by God, discrowned by man!)
The hated flag of red and white and green.

When was thy glory! when in search for power
Thine eagles flew to greet the double sun,
And all the nations trembled at thy rod?
Nay, but thy glory tarried for this hour,
When pilgrims kneel before the Holy One,
The prisoned shepherd of the Church of God.

– 神聖永恆之城 –

羅馬！你的歷史卷軸雄偉壯觀，
自帝國濫觴，你用共和國的劍
統御世界，世世代代延綿不絕：
你的人民為你加冕為后，
直到街上來了蓄鬚髯的歌德人；
如今微風輕輕吹拂著你的城牆
（啊，上帝加冕的城，人民摘冠之國！）
紅白綠相間的國旗，備受怨憎。

榮耀光輝已不再！你追逐權勢
你的老鷹翱翔高空，迎接雙日，
所有國度仍在你威權下顫巍巍？
不，但榮耀停留於此刻此時，
朝聖者雙膝跪在神聖真主前，
上帝殿堂裡遭禁錮的牧羊人[6]。

– Sonnet on Hearing the Dies Iræ Sung – in the Sistine Chapel

Nay, Lord, not thus! white lilies in the spring,
Sad olive-groves, or silver-breasted dove,
Teach me more clearly of Thy life and love
Than terrors of red flame and thundering.
The hillside vines dear memories of Thee bring:
A bird at evening flying to its nest,
Tells me of One who had no place of rest:
I think it is of Thee the sparrows sing.
Come rather on some autumn afternoon,
When red and brown are burnished on the leaves,
And the fields echo to the gleaner's song,
Come when the splendid fulness of the moon
Looks down upon the rows of golden sheaves,
And reap Thy harvest: we have waited long.

- 西斯汀教堂響起的最後審判讚美詩 -

不，主啊，非也！春季的白百合，
哀戚的橄欖園，或銀白胸膛的鴿，
對我細數訴說祢的愛與生
勝過赤紅烈焰和隆隆雷聲的威嚇。
山陵藤蔓帶來關於祢的美妙回憶：
一隻在黯黑夜晚歸巢的鳥，
對我傾訴，祂遍尋不著安居處所：
麻雀哼唱的，我認為是祢。
不如選在秋日午後降臨吧，
紅棕樹葉閃爍發亮的季節，
田野裡迴盪起拾穗者之歌，
在滿月如鏡的時刻降臨吧，
月兒俯視著黃金稻穗收割，
亦收穫祢的成果：我們已等到花謝。

〈灰與黑的改編曲：畫家的母親〉
(Arrangement in Grey and Black: Portrait of the Painter's Mother, 1871)
畫中人物為安娜・惠斯勒。

– Ave Maria Plena Gratia –

Was this His coming! I had hoped to see
A scene of wondrous glory, as was told
Of some great God who in a rain of gold
Broke open bars and fell on Danae:
Or a dread vision as when Semele
Sickening for love and unappeased desire
Prayed to see God's clear body, and the fire
Caught her white limbs and slew her utterly:
With such glad dreams I sought this holy place,
And now with wondering eyes and heart I stand
Before this supreme mystery of Love:
A kneeling girl with passionless pale face,
An angel with a lily in his hand,
And over both with outstretched wings the Dove.

– 慈悲的瑪利亞萬歲 –

難道會是祂的降臨！我冀盼目睹
榮耀光景，一如
偉大天神，化身黃金雨
攻破門欄，降於達妮的寓言：
抑或施美樂[7]見到的可怖景象
為愛情茶飯不思，為慾望騷動不止
僅祈求凝望天神的雷電之軀，奪命的
電光石火，吻上她潔白身軀：
如此旖旎夢境，我尋覓神聖之地，
帶著游移雙眼，浮動的心，
我站在愛情的崇高祕密前：
容顏蒼白無神的女孩跪地，
天使手裡托著百合，
這兩人頭頂，一隻白鴿展開雙翼。

7　希臘神話典故。凡人公主施美樂要求情人宙斯以真實的神光示人，後來因承受不了炙熱雷霆而
　　死去。

– The Grave of Shelley –

Like burnt-out torches by a sick man's bed
Gaunt cypress-trees stand round the sun-bleached stone;
Here doth the little night-owl make her throne,
And the slight lizard show his jewelled head.
And, where the chaliced poppies flame to red,
In the still chamber of yon pyramid
Surely some Old-World Sphinx lurks darkly hid,
Grim warder of this pleasaunce of the dead.

Ah! sweet indeed to rest within the womb
Of Earth, great mother of eternal sleep,
But sweeter far for thee a restless tomb
In the blue cavern of an echoing deep,
Or where the tall ships founder in the gloom
Against the rocks of some wave-shattered steep.

− 雪萊之墓 [8] −

臨終男人床畔般，火炬燃燒殆盡，
高瘦柏樹矗立於太陽炙烤的白石；
夜裡小貓頭鷹登上寶座，
小蜥蜴露出的頭顱彷如鑲上寶石。
聖餐杯般的罌粟，如烈焰般火紅，
遠方金字塔的寧靜房間，
舊世界的人面獅身獸黑暗裡蟄伏，
對亡者感到油然愉悅的無情獄吏。

啊！歸於塵土的墳墓固然甜美，
大地是永恆之眠的偉大母親，
對你，永不沉睡的墳墓更美，
在深處回聲盪漾的深藍洞窟，
聳高船隻衝撞浪擊的峭壁礁岩
沉沒陷入昏暗之中。

8　英國浪漫主義詩人雪萊（Percy Shelley, 1792-1822），三十歲那年離開義大利海岸時，因為一場暴
　　風雨受困拉斯佩奇亞海灣（Gulf of La Spezia）附近，數日後他和船上人員的遺體被沖刷上岸。

– Santa Decca –

The Gods are dead: no longer do we bring
To grey-eyed Pallas crowns of olive-leaves!
Demeter's child no more hath tithe of sheaves,
And in the noon the careless shepherds sing,
For Pan is dead, and all the wantoning
By secret glade and devious haunt is o'er:
Young Hylas seeks the water-springs no more;
Great Pan is dead, and Mary's Son is King.

And yet—perchance in this sea-trancèd isle,
Chewing the bitter fruit of memory,
Some God lies hidden in the asphodel.
Ah Love! if such there be then it were well
For us to fly his anger: nay, but see
The leaves are stirring: let us watch a-while.

– 聖德卡山 –

諸神已歿：不再為
灰眼雅典娜加冕橄欖葉皇冠！
狄美特[9]子女亦莫再享什一稅[10]，
正午時分，牧羊人悠遊哼唱，
因潘神[11]已亡，不再胡作非為，
祕密林地和不當狩獵告終：
年輕海拉斯[12]不再尋覓泉水；
偉大潘神已死，瑪利亞之子登基為王。

然而——若偶然在這座大海迷茫的小島，
咀嚼著回憶的苦澀果實，
天神就藏匿在常春花裡。
啊，是愛神！若正巧如此亦好，
我們逃離他的震怒：不，且看
樹葉在搖曳：讓咱們再次凝望。

9　掌管農業與穀物的女神。

10　歐洲基督教會利用十分之一農牧產品屬於上帝的聖經說法，向農民徵收什一稅。

11　牧神，照顧牧羊人、獵人、農人與鄉野人民的希臘神祇。

12　希臘神話的美男子，為海克力士的伴侶，跟著海克力士參加金羊毛遠征時，被海妖愛上劫走。

– Magdalen Walks –

The little white clouds are racing over the sky,
And the fields are strewn with the gold of the flower of March,
The daffodil breaks under foot, and the tasselled larch
Sways and swings as the thrush goes hurrying by.

A delicate odour is borne on the wings of the morning breeze,
The odour of deep wet grass, and of brown new-furrowed earth,
The birds are singing for joy of the Spring's glad birth,
Hopping from branch to branch on the rocking trees.

And all the woods are alive with the murmur and sound of Spring,
And the rose-bud breaks into pink on the climbing briar,
And the crocus-bed is a quivering moon of fire
Girdled round with the belt of an amethyst ring.

And the plane to the pine-tree is whispering some tale of love
Till it rustles with laughter and tosses its mantle of green,
And the gloom of the wych-elm's hollow is lit with the iris sheen
Of the burnished rainbow throat and the silver breast of a dove.

See! the lark starts up from his bed in the meadow there,
Breaking the gossamer threads and the nets of dew,
And flashing adown the river, a flame of blue!
The kingfisher flies like an arrow, and wounds the air.

– 漫步莫德林[13] –

嬌小白花花雲朵，天空一閃而逝，
田野遍灑三月花朵的金黃，
黃水仙分離腳下，歌鶇振翅倉皇
落葉松禾穗隨著左搖右晃。

優雅芬芳乘著清晨微風的雙翼，
濡濕青草芬芳，初耕褐土香氣，
鳥兒歡天喜地歌頌著春季誕生，
在搖曳樹木枝椏間，蹦蹦跳跳。

森林活躍地飄散著春語喃喃，
玫瑰花苞在攀藤上綻放紅粉，
花棚床是顫抖的火紅滿月，
圍繞著紫水晶花圈的腰帶。

松樹的平頂正輕聲訴說著愛情寓言
直到窸窣笑語，掀開它綠油油的斗篷，
鴿子閃亮耀眼的虹彩喉頭與銀白胸口，
彩色光芒點亮了無毛榆的漆黑空洞。

看啊！雲雀在牠草地小床甦醒，
劃破露水點點的蛛絲網及細線，
低空閃逝至河邊，如藍色火焰！
翠鳥彷若飛射箭頭，刺傷空氣。

13　自都柏林聖三一大學（Trinity College）畢業後，王爾德獲得英國牛津大學莫德林學院的半院士獎
　　學金，這首是他獻給母校的小詩。

– Theocritus: A Villanelle –

O singer of Persephone!
In the dim meadows desolate
Dost thou remember Sicily?

Still through the ivy flits the bee
Where Amaryllis lies in state;
O Singer of Persephone!

Simaetha calls on Hecate
And hears the wild dogs at the gate;
Dost thou remember Sicily?

Still by the light and laughing sea
Poor Polypheme bemoans his fate;
O Singer of Persephone!

And still in boyish rivalry
Young Daphnis challenges his mate;
Dost thou remember Sicily?

– 席奧客里特斯 [14]：田園詩 –

噢，吟唱波塞芬妮 [15] 的詩人！
那荒蕪陰鬱草地裡
你是否記得西西里？

蜜蜂輕盈安靜掠過常春藤，
孤挺花幽幽躺著；
噢，吟唱波塞芬妮的詩人！

西邁塔蛛叩見黑卡蒂 [16]，
猶聞門前的守衛惡犬；
你是否記得西西里？

依然逗留日光與呼嘯大海，
可憐波利菲莫斯 [17] 哀嘆命運；
噢，吟唱波塞芬妮的詩人！

青春正旺的叛逆，
年輕氣盛的達夫尼 [18] 挑戰同伴；
你是否記得西西里？

---

14 古希臘詩人，亦是西方田園詩歌的創始人。

15 春天與大地女神，遭到地府之神黑帝斯擄至地底當新娘，每年某個時段，可以回到大地。

16 希臘神話中的地獄女神。

17 《尤里西斯》裡，遭漂流小島的奧德修斯戳瞎眼的獨眼巨人。

18 希臘神話裡的愛情故事《達夫尼和克羅伊》主角，兩人為了結合，排除萬難，接下各種挑戰冒險，最後得償所願。

纖瘦拉孔 [19] 為你顧了頭山羊，
快樂的牧羊人正在守候你；
噢，吟唱波塞芬妮的詩人！
你是否記得西西里？

Slim Lacon keeps a goat for thee,
For thee the jocund shepherds wait;
O Singer of Persephone!
Dost thou remember Sicily?

---

19 西元前二世紀的伊比鳩魯派哲學家，歌頌精神與肉體歡愉的享樂主義者。

〈黑與金的夜曲：煙火〉
（ Nocturne in Black and Gold: The Falling Rocket, 1875 ）

– Endymion –

The apple trees are hung with gold,
And birds are loud in Arcady,
The sheep lie bleating in the fold,
The wild goat runs across the wold,
But yesterday his love he told,
I know he will come back to me.
O rising moon! O Lady moon!
Be you my lover's sentinel,
You cannot choose but know him well,
For he is shod with purple shoon,
You cannot choose but know my love,
For he a shepherd's crook doth bear,
And he is soft as any dove,
And brown and curly is his hair.

The turtle now has ceased to call
Upon her crimson-footed groom,
The grey wolf prowls about the stall,
The lily's singing seneschal
Sleeps in the lily-bell, and all
The violet hills are lost in gloom.
O risen moon! O holy moon!
Stand on the top of Helice,
And if my own true love you see,

－ 恩底彌翁 [20] －

蘋果樹上懸掛金黃，
阿卡迪的鳥兒喋喋，
起伏山谷，羊兒咩咩，
野山羊奔過了原野，
昨日他向愛人承諾，
我知他會回來找我。
噢，冉冉高升的月！噢，月亮女神！
你是我愛人的守護神，
你不得不熟知他，
因他腳上亦踩雙紫鞋，
你不得不熟知我愛人，
因他持牧羊人曲柄杖，
性情溫吞如鴿，
髮絲黃褐鬈曲。

烏龜終於不再呼喊
她棕紅四肢的新郎，
灰狼馬廄周遭徘徊，
百合那哼歌的管家
在百合花圃裡沉睡，
昏暗中不見紫羅蘭山坡。
噢，躍升的月！噢，神聖的月！
懸空立在海利斯城高處，
若你遇見我的真愛，

---

20 希臘神話裡，月亮女神西倫愛上恩底彌翁，於是請求宙斯應允他想要的東西，恩底彌翁選擇長
　　眠，青春不老。

Ah! if you see the purple shoon,
The hazel crook, the lad's brown hair,
The goat-skin wrapped about his arm,
Tell him that I am waiting where
The rushlight glimmers in the Farm.

The falling dew is cold and chill,
And no bird sings in Arcady,
The little fauns have left the hill,
Even the tired daffodil
Has closed its gilded doors, and still
My lover comes not back to me.
False moon! False moon! O waning moon!
Where is my own true lover gone,
Where are the lips vermilion,
The shepherd's crook, the purple shoon?
Why spread that silver pavilion,
Why wear that veil of drifting mist?
Ah! thou hast young Endymion,
Thou hast the lips that should be kissed!

啊！倘若瞥見那雙紫鞋，
榛木曲柄杖，男孩褐髮，
披繞胳膊的山羊皮，
告訴他，我在農場裡
闌珊燈火旁守候著他。

滾落的露水冰寒透心，
阿卡迪的鳥兒不歌唱，
小小牧神離開丘陵，
就連疲憊的黃水仙
都闔起它鍍金大門，而
我的愛人，卻始終不回來。
假面的月！虛偽的月！噢，削瘦缺月！
我的真愛去了哪兒？
豔紅嘴唇究竟何方？
牧羊人的曲柄杖、紫鞋在哪？
你怎麼會撐開銀白色的天篷？
你為何披掛飄渺迷霧的面紗？
啊！你奪走青春的恩底彌翁，
你佔有那兩瓣值得親吻的唇！

– Ballade de Marguerite (Normande) –

I am weary of lying within the chase
When the knights are meeting in market-place.

Nay, go not thou to the red-roofed town
Lest the hoofs of the war-horse tread thee down.

But I would not go where the Squires ride,
I would only walk by my Lady's side.

Alack! and alack! thou art overbold,
A Forester's son may not eat off gold.

Will she love me the less that my Father is seen
Each Martinmas day in a doublet green?

Perchance she is sewing at tapestrie,
Spindle and loom are not meet for thee.

Ah, if she is working the arras bright
I might ravel the threads by the fire-light.

Perchance she is hunting of the deer,
How could you follow o'er hill and mere?

Ah, if she is riding with the court,
I might run beside her and wind the morte.

– 瑪格麗特敘事曲（諾曼第）–

追逐令我精疲力竭，
騎士約在市集相會。

不，別去紅屋頂小鎮，
戰馬的蹄會將你踐踏。

但我不去屈從那兒，
只會走在夫人身旁。

嗚呼！哀哉！你魯莽膽大，
森林居民之子不穿金戴銀。

若有人在聖馬丁節，瞥見我父
戴綠寶石，她是否會減損我的愛？

她偶然繡著錦絨，
紡錘與織布機不為你相逢。

啊，倘若她織起豔麗花毯，
我就在那燈火旁鬆開絲線。

她偶爾亦會獵鹿，
你要如何攀山越湖跟上路？

啊，若她與廷臣騎馬，
我將在一旁氣喘吁吁。

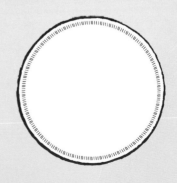

Perchance she is kneeling in St. Denys,
(On her soul may our Lady have gramercy!)

Ah, if she is praying in lone chapelle,
I might swing the censer and ring the bell.

Come in, my son, for you look sae pale,
The father shall fill thee a stoup of ale.

But who are these knights in bright array?
Is it a pageant the rich folks play?

'T is the King of England from over sea,
Who has come unto visit our fair countrie.

But why does the curfew toll sae low?
And why do the mourners walk a-row?

O 't is Hugh of Amiens my sister's son
Who is lying stark, for his day is done.

Nay, nay, for I see white lilies clear,
It is no strong man who lies on the bier.

O 't is old Dame Jeannette that kept the hall,
I knew she would die at the autumn fall.

她偶爾在聖丹尼斯[21]跪拜，
（盼望著靈魂獲得赦免！）

啊，倘若她在孤獨教堂祈禱，
我也許會擺盪香爐，敲響鐘聲。

進來吧，我的兒，你一臉蒼白，
父親將為你倒杯麥酒。

但盛裝列陣的騎士是誰？
難不成是富人列隊遊行？

是飄洋過海的英格蘭國王，
來到我們美麗的鄉間巡訪。

那晚鐘為何敲得幽沉？
為何哀悼者列隊前進？

噢，那是亞眠的休[22]，妹妹的兒，
蒙主恩召，肢體僵硬躺在那兒。

不，不，我看見了淨白百合，
躺在棺架的人並不身強體壯。

噢，那是守護門廳的珍內女士，
我知道她將在秋臨之時殞歿。

---

21 位於英格蘭東南區域的南開普頓。
22 十二世紀的法國克呂尼修士，著有許多詩詞、聖經註釋，及最早的系統神學理論專著。

Dame Jeannette had not that gold-brown hair,
Old Jeannette was not a maiden fair.

O 't is none of our kith and none of our kin,
(Her soul may our Lady assoil from sin!)

But I hear the boy's voice chaunting sweet,
'Elle est morte, la Marguerite.'

Come in, my son, and lie on the bed,
And let the dead folk bury their dead.

O mother, you know I loved her true:
O mother, hath one grave room for two?

珍內女士沒有金棕秀髮，
老珍內非似玉如花少女。

噢，那不是我們的親人摯友，
（願聖母赦免她的靈魂！）

然我聽聞男孩哼著甜美歌聲，
「她已死亡，瑪格麗特。」

進來，我的兒，躺上床，
讓死者埋葬他們的死亡。

噢，母親，你知道我對她的愛如真：
噢，母親，一座墳可否容下兩個人？

– The New Helen –

Where hast thou been since round the walls of Troy
The sons of God fought in that great emprise?
Why dost thou walk our common earth again?
Hast thou forgotten that impassioned boy,
His purple galley, and his Tyrian men,
And treacherous Aphrodite's mocking eyes?
For surely it was thou, who, like a star
Hung in the silver silence of the night,
Didst lure the Old World's chivalry and might
Into the clamorous crimson waves of war!

Or didst thou rule the fire-laden moon?
In amorous Sidon was thy temple built
Over the light and laughter of the sea?
Where, behind lattice scarlet-wrought and gilt,
Some brown-limbed girl did weave thee tapestry,
All through the waste and wearied hours of noon;
Till her wan cheek with flame of passion burned,
And she rose up the sea-washed lips to kiss
Of some glad Cyprian sailor, safe returned
From Calpé and the cliffs of Herakles!

– 嶄新的海倫 –

上帝之子，冒著生命危險，
特洛伊城牆外，烽火連年，
你在哪兒？怎能再度漫步凡塵？
難道你忘懷那滿腔熱情的男孩，
他的紫色軍艦，他的蒂爾人民，
以及愛芙蘿黛提[23] 詭變的睥睨？
自然是你，猶如星辰
高掛於深夜銀色寂靜，
魅惑舊世界的騎士和力量
踏進干戈不息的血腥狂浪！

抑或，你掌管著光火通明的圓月？
在情意綿綿的西頓城，那屬於你的神殿
建蓋在高懸海洋的微光與笑語上？
在暗紅與鍍金精緻交織的柵格背後，
棕膚女子為你編織著繡帷，
荒蕪的正午使人昏昏欲睡；
直到她削瘦的臉頰，燃燒熱情焰火，
她噘起海水洗禮的唇一吻
那名塞普勒斯的得意水手，
自卡爾佩[24] 和海克力斯的懸崖[25] 平安返歸。

---

23 希臘神話中，代表美麗、愛與性的女神。
24 西班牙東邊的城鎮，鄰近地中海。
25 摩洛哥的海克力斯洞穴懸崖，隔著直布羅陀海峽對望西班牙南方。

No! thou art Helen, and none other one!
It was for thee that young Sarpedôn died,
And Memnôn's manhood was untimely spent;
It was for thee gold-crested Hector tried
With Thetis' child that evil race to run,
In the last year of thy beleaguerment;
Ay! even now the glory of thy fame
Burns in those fields of trampled asphodel,
Where the high lords whom Ilion knew so well
Clash ghostly shields, and call upon thy name.

Where hast thou been? in that enchanted land
Whose slumbering vales forlorn Calypso knew,
Where never mower rose to greet the day
But all unswathed the trammelling grasses grew,
And the sad shepherd saw the tall corn stand
Till summer's red had changed to withered gray?
Didst thou lie there by some Lethæan stream
Deep brooding on thine ancient memory,
The crash of broken spears, the fiery gleam
From shivered helm, the Grecian battle-cry.

不！正是你海倫，別無他人！
為了你，薩皮東 [26] 英年早逝，
門儂 [27] 的壯年生命亦及早收場；
為了你，金黃頭盔的赫克特
亦在你多事紛擾的最終那年，
與佘蒂絲之子 [28] 邪惡交戰，
對！一如現在，你的盛名
在黃水仙踐踏的平原燃燒，
伊利昂 [29] 最熟悉這裡的君主，
盾牌鬼影衝撞，喚著你名。

你去了哪裡？在蠱惑的土地
孤零零的卡麗騷 [30] 熟悉的沉睡山谷，
收割人從未早起迎接嶄新一天，
未綑綁束縛的野草漫天生長，
悲傷牧羊人望小麥高聳而立
直到夏日豔紅，萎靡成灰？
你是否就躺在那遺忘河畔
鬱鬱寡歡沉思著古老記憶，
破碎戰矛的落地鏗鏘，
顫抖的船舵柄閃爍，發出希臘戰爭呼喊。

---

26 特洛伊的第二勇將。
27 特洛伊國王。
28 阿基里斯，特洛伊第一勇將赫克特的摯友。
29 位於希臘雅典近郊。
30 希臘神話中的海之女神，奧德修斯以木馬屠城計攻破特洛伊城後，返家路途迷航，停留在卡麗
　　騷的小島，她則將他困在島上七年之久。

Nay, thou wert hidden in that hollow hill
With one who is forgotten utterly,
That discrowned Queen men call the Erycine;
Hidden away that never mightst thou see
The face of Her, before whose mouldering shrine
To-day at Rome the silent nations kneel;
Who gat from Love no joyous gladdening,
But only Love's intolerable pain,
Only a sword to pierce her heart in twain,
Only the bitterness of child-bearing.

The lotos-leaves which heal the wounds of Death
Lie in thy hand; O, be thou kind to me,
While yet I know the summer of my days;
For hardly can my tremulous lips draw breath
To fill the silver trumpet with thy praise,
So bowed am I before thy mystery;
So bowed and broken on Love's terrible wheel,
That I have lost all hope and heart to sing,
Yet care I not what ruin time may bring
If in thy temple thou wilt let me kneel.

Alas, alas, thou wilt not tarry here,
But, like that bird, the servant of the sun,
Who flies before the northwind and the night,
So wilt thou fly our evil land and drear,
Back to the tower of thine old delight,

不，你與舉世遺忘的她，
人人口中的罷黜皇后，
厄律辛納 [31]，藏在空壑山陵；
躲在永不見她臉龐之處，
在她坍塌腐朽的神龕前
沉默國度在羅馬跟前跪下；
他們未從愛獲得愉悅滿足，
唯獨愛情難以承受的痛楚，
唯將她心撕裂成半的利劍，
唯有孕育子女的酸澀苦楚。

治療痙癒死者之殤的蓮葉
就在你掌心；噢，請對我溫柔，
趁我尚能體會人生盛夏，
只因我顫抖的唇不能呼吸，
用你的讚美填滿銀色號角。
我在你的神祕面前彎下腰；
愛神恐懼之輪彎折壓碎我，
我已喪失希望和歌唱之心，
但我不在乎時光帶來破壞，
只求你讓我跪在你神殿裡。

嗚呼，嗚呼，你不在此停歇，
卻如那隻鳥，太陽的僕人，
北風黑夜降臨前振翅奔飛，
請將我們的邪惡陰鬱大地
送回你那古老愉悅的高塔，

---

31 西西里島埃塞克斯山的愛神。

And the red lips of young Euphorion;
Nor shall I ever see thy face again,
But in this poisonous garden must I stay,
Crowning my brows with the thorn-crown of pain,
Till all my loveless life shall pass away.

O Helen! Helen! Helen! yet awhile,
Yet for a little while, O, tarry here,
Till the dawn cometh and the shadows flee!
For in the gladsome sunlight of thy smile
Of heaven or hell I have no thought or fear,
Seeing I know no other god but thee:
No other god save him, before whose feet
In nets of gold the tired planets move,
The incarnate spirit of spiritual love
Who in thy body holds his joyous seat.

Thou wert not born as common women are!
But, girt with silver splendour of the foam,
Didst from the depths of sapphire seas arise!
And at thy coming some immortal star,
Bearded with flame, blazed in the Eastern skies,
And waked the shepherds on thine island-home.
Thou shalt not die: no asps of Egypt creep
Close at thy heels to taint the delicate air;
No sullen-blooming poppies stain thy hair,
Those scarlet heralds of eternal sleep.

返回氣盛的尤佛里安 [32] 紅唇；
我再也不會看見你的面容，
然我必須留守這劇毒花園，
讓荊棘的痛苦皇冠扣上眉，
直到空洞無愛的人生逝去。

噢，海倫！海倫！海倫！
噢，別走，請再停留片刻，
直到黎明破曉，黑影溜走！
唯在你微笑的愉悅日光裡
我才能不思不懼天堂地獄，
因你是我唯一知悉的神祇：
沒有神解救他，倦累的星體
在他纏裹黃金網的腳前移動，
他是心靈之愛的精神化身，
在你體內他保有一席喜樂。

你生來即非平凡女子！
銀白潔亮泡沫圍繞你身，
從藍寶石大海深處躍升！
你的降臨猶如不朽之星，
火焰紋身，在東方天際燃燒，
在你的家鄉小島驚醒牧羊人。
你不該死：埃及角蝰未潛爬
至你的腳踝，玷汙潔淨氣息；
陰鬱盛開的罌粟，永眠的鮮紅使者，
亦不得汙染你的髮。

---

32 在《浮士德》中，浮士德與海倫兩人狂傲不羈的愛子墜海而亡。

愛情的百合，純潔不可侵！
象牙白塔！火紅玫瑰！
你降臨黑暗，照亮萬物：
只因我們糾結在遼闊的命運之網，
疲累地等候人間欲望降臨，
漫無目的遊蕩在陰暗殿堂，
漫無目的尋覓睡眠的解藥，
為了頹廢荒蕪的生命，為了久不消逝的不幸，
直到我們凝望你再度登場的神龕，
以及你美好的純白榮耀。

Lily of love, pure and inviolate!
Tower of ivory! red rose of fire!
Thou hast come down our darkness to illume:
For we, close-caught in the wide nets of Fate,
Wearied with waiting for the World's Desire,
Aimlessly wandered in the house of gloom,
Aimlessly sought some slumberous anodyne
For wasted lives, for lingering wretchedness,
Till we beheld thy re-arisen shrine,
And the white glory of thy loveliness.

〈珍珠與銀的母親：安達魯西亞人〉
（Mother of Pearl and Silver: The Andalusian, 1888-90）
畫中模特兒為惠特曼妻子之妹，坎塞爾。

– Madonna Mia –

A lily-girl, not made for this world's pain,
With brown, soft hair close braided by her ears,
And longing eyes half veiled by slumberous tears
Like bluest water seen through mists of rain:
Pale cheeks whereon no love hath left its stain,
Red underlip drawn in for fear of love,
And white throat, whiter than the silvered dove,
Through whose wan marble creeps one purple vein.

Yet, though my lips shall praise her without cease,
Even to kiss her feet I am not bold,
Being o'ershadowed by the wings of awe.
Like Dante, when he stood with Beatrice
Beneath the flaming Lion's breast, and saw
The seventh Crystal, and the Stair of Gold.

- 我的聖母 -

百合般的女孩，不識人間疾苦，
柔軟褐髮密實編紮耳畔，
睡夢般的淚水半掩著渴望雙眼
恍若雨霧朦朧下，最湛藍海水：
沒有吻曾留下痕跡的蒼白面頰，
恐懼著愛，緊咬下唇，
皓白喉頭，白過銀鴿，
黯淡大理石表面爬過深紫血管。

雖然我的唇應永不停歇讚美她，
即使是親吻她的腳，都不勇敢，
敬畏的雙翅，為我籠罩於陰影。
一如但丁，與貝緹麗彩站立在
那火焰熊熊的雄獅胸口下
望見第七顆水晶，上帝的階梯。

– Roses and Rue –

I remember we used to meet
By an ivied seat,
And you warbled each pretty word
With the air of a bird;

And your voice had a quaver in it,
Just like a linnet,
And shook, as the blackbird's throat
With its last big note;

And your eyes, they were green and grey
Like an April day,
But lit into amethyst
When I stooped and kissed;

And your mouth, it would never smile
For a long, long while,
Then it rippled all over with laughter
Five minutes after.

You were always afraid of a shower,
Just like a flower:
I remember you started and ran
When the rain began.

I remember I never could catch you,
For no one could match you,

– 薔薇與芸香 –

猶記我們曾約在常春藤
織繞的椅上相逢，
你用鳥兒的樂曲
囀鳴出每一個悅耳字句；

你的聲音帶著一股顫動，
彷若紅雀，
猶如烏鶇喉頭發出輕顫，
最終飄出高昂音符；

你的眼，既翠且灰，
好似四月天，
我屈身親吻
卻化為燃燒紫水晶；

而你的嘴，長久不曾
掛著的笑容，
笑聲蕩漾出漣漪
足足五分鐘。

你總懼怕陣雨，
一如花朵：
猶記雨紛落時
你即拔腿跑走。

我記得，我捉不著你，
沒人匹配得上你，

You had wonderful, luminous, fleet,
Little wings to your feet.

I remember your hair — did I tie it?
For it always ran riot —
Like a tangled sunbeam of gold:
These things are old.

I remember so well the room,
And the lilac bloom
That beat at the dripping pane
In the warm June rain;

And the colour of your gown,
It was amber-brown,
And two yellow satin bows
From the shoulders rose.

And the handkerchief of French lace
Which you held to your face —
Had a small tear left a stain?
Or was it the rain?

On your hand as it waved adieu
There were veins of blue;
In your voice as it said good-bye
Was a petulant cry,

"You have only wasted your life."
(Ah, that was the knife!)

你的雙足像長了翅膀，
美妙光彩的飛掠。

我記得你的髮——我可曾繫綁？
總是凌亂紛飛——
好比糾結的黃金日光：
皆已歷史悠長。

我還記得那間房，
紫丁香芬芳綻放
在暖意的六月雨
叮咚拍打著窗櫺；

你衣袍的色彩，
是琥珀色澤，
兩朵黃色緞結
從肩頭竄起。

法國蕾絲手帕
用來遮蓋面容——
淚珠留下淚痕？
抑或只是雨水？

你搖著手告別，
爬著幾絡靛藍；
臨別再會聲音
是你任性呼喊。

「你平白浪費一生。」
（啊，這話銳如利刃！）

When I rushed through the garden gate
It was all too late.

Could we live it over again,
Were it worth the pain,
Could the passionate past that is fled
Call back its dead!

Well, if my heart must break,
Dear love, for your sake,
It will break in music, I know,
Poets' hearts break so.

But strange that I was not told
That the brain can hold
In a tiny ivory cell
God's heaven and hell.

我俯衝過花園大門
卻為時已晚。

我們能否再活一遍，
疼痛是否真的值得，
已流逝的熱情過往
能否喚醒逝去歲月！

倘若我心必須破碎，
親愛情人，為了你，
我知必碎在樂音裡，
這就是詩人的心碎。

奇異的是，我沒聽說
腦海裡竟有一席之地
在那微小的象牙房裡，
關著上帝的天堂地獄。

〈陽台〉（The Balcony, 1879-80）
惠斯勒於威尼斯所繪的陽台街景。

－ 波西亞 ³³ －

不為巴薩尼奧的英勇驚呼，
不為他冒風險選鉛盒讚嘆，
抑或驕傲的阿拉貢親王垂下頭，
或是摩洛哥親王熾熱的心冷卻：
只因那黃金打造的華服
比金黃色澤的太陽金光更閃耀，
我仰望的維洛納女子
沒有人的美，可及我眼中的你。
但你穿戴著樸實律師袍，
那智慧護罩，甚至更美，
不甘威尼斯律法擊敗安東尼奧，
他的真心不得輸給可惡猶太人——
噢，波西亞！帶走我的心：這顆心是你的：
我想我不會為了抵押鬥嘴。

－ Portia －

I marvel not Bassanio was so bold
To peril all he had upon the lead,
Or that proud Aragon bent low his head,
Or that Morocco's fiery heart grew cold:
For in that gorgeous dress of beaten gold

33　王爾德將此詩獻給在《威尼斯商人》飾演波西亞的英國著名女演員艾倫‧泰瑞（Ellen Terry），歌
　　頌她在劇中的演技與美貌。

Which is more golden than the golden sun,
No woman Veronesé looked upon
Was half so fair as thou whom I behold.
Yet fairer when with wisdom as your shield
The sober-suited lawyer's gown you donned
And would not let the laws of Venice yield
Antonio's heart to that accursèd Jew—
O Portia! take my heart: it is thy due:
I think I will not quarrel with the Bond.

〈粉色與灰色的和聲：謬克斯女士的肖像〉
(Harmony in Pink and Grey: Portrait of Lady Meux, 1881)

– Quia Multum Amavi –

Dear Heart I think the young impassioned priest
When first he takes from out the hidden shrine
His God imprisoned in the Eucharist,
And eats the bread, and drinks the dreadful wine,

Feels not such awful wonder as I felt
When first my smitten eyes beat full on thee,
And all night long before thy feet I knelt
Till thou wert wearied of Idolatry.

Ah! had'st thou liked me less and loved me more,
Through all those summer days of joy and rain,
I had not now been sorrow's heritor,
Or stood a lackey in the House of Pain.

Yet, though remorse, youth's white-faced seneschal
Tread on my heels with all his retinue,
I am most glad I loved thee—think of all
The suns that go to make one speedwell blue!

– 因為她愛過 –

親愛的心，青春熱情牧師
自藏匿聖餐裡的神龕
首度介紹禁錮的上帝，
嚼著麵包，啜著敬畏的酒，

我神魂顛倒的眼初次落在你身
卻感覺不到，令人敬畏的奇蹟，
我徹夜跪在你面前
直到偶像崇拜倦累。

啊！若你的喜歡較淺，愛卻深，
每一個喜悅與雨水的盛夏日子，
我現在就不會是個哀愁的嗣子，
更不會是哀痛殿堂裡的奴僕。

而雖然痛悔，青春的慘白管家
跟著他的扈從，隨我後腳跟走，
我愛過你，我很知足──請想想
那把婆婆納花曬得靛藍的千陽！

– Silentium Amoris –

As oftentimes the too resplendent sun
Hurries the pallid and reluctant moon
Back to her sombre cave, ere she hath won
A single ballad from the nightingale,
So doth thy Beauty make my lips to fail,
And all my sweetest singing out of tune.

And as at dawn across the level mead
On wings impetuous some wind will come,
And with its too harsh kisses break the reed
Which was its only instrument of song,
So my too stormy passions work me wrong,
And for excess of Love my Love is dumb.

But surely unto Thee mine eyes did show
Why I am silent, and my lute unstrung;
Else it were better we should part, and go,
Thou to some lips of sweeter melody,
And I to nurse the barren memory
Of unkissed kisses, and songs never sung.

－ 愛的沉默 －

燦爛豔陽，聲聲催促
那蒼憂不情願的月娘
贏得夜鶯一曲情歌前，
歸返至她的幽影巢穴，
你的美貌我啞口無言，
我甜蜜嗓音哼不成調。

黎明時分，在水平線的草原
風兒乘著它的狂暴翅膀抵達，
它粗暴的熱吻，壓垮了蘆葦，
這是它演奏曲目的唯一樂器，
我亦錯用我過於狂野的熱情，
愛得過火，我的愛麻木僵硬。

而我望著你的眼真實訴說
為何我靜默，而詩琴無語；
但我們還是分道揚鑣的好，
你去找甜美旋律的唇，
我則去孕育枯乏回憶，
追思未吻的吻，未歌之歌。

– Her Voice –

The wild bee reels from bough to bough
With his furry coat and his gauzy wing.
Now in a lily-cup, and now
Setting a jacinth bell a-swing,
In his wandering;
Sit closer love: it was here I trow
I made that vow,

Swore that two lives should be like one
As long as the sea-gull loved the sea,
As long as the sunflower sought the sun,—
It shall be, I said, for eternity
'Twixt you and me!
Dear friend, those times are over and done,
Love's web is spun.

Look upward where the poplar trees
Sway and sway in the summer air,
Here in the valley never a breeze
Scatters the thistledown, but there
Great winds blow fair
From the mighty murmuring mystical seas,
And the wave-lashed leas.

– 她的聲音 –

穿著蓬毛外衣，似紗翅膀，
野蜂在樹枝間，翩然旋舞。
他悠遊漫舞，一會兒
在百合花托，一會兒
輕輕搖晃風信子的鈴；
坐過來，我的愛：我想
我就是在這兒訂下誓言。

誓言兩人要合而為一，
只要海鷗依舊愛著大海，
只要向日葵仍尋覓太陽，——
我說，你我之間
這種愛便是永恆！
親愛朋友，時光褪色消逝，
愛情網亦已編織。

舉頭仰望白楊樹
在夏日微風裡，輕盈搖擺，
在這兒的山谷，微風從不
吹散薊花冠毛，但在那兒
強風白喃喃浩瀚的神祕海
以及海浪拍打的大草原上，
美妙吹送著。

Look upward where the white gull screams,
What does it see that we do not see?
Is that a star? or the lamp that gleams
On some outward voyaging argosy,—
Ah! can it be
We have lived our lives in a land of dreams!
How sad it seems.

Sweet, there is nothing left to say
But this, that love is never lost,
Keen winter stabs the breasts of May
Whose crimson roses burst his frost,
Ships tempest-tossed
Will find a harbour in some bay,
And so we may.

And there is nothing left to do
But to kiss once again, and part,
Nay, there is nothing we should rue,
I have my beauty,—you your Art,
Nay, do not start,
One world was not enough for two
Like me and you.

舉頭仰望尖叫的潔白海鷗，
牠看到什麼我們不察之物？
是星辰？遠方航行的大船、
曖曖閃耀的燈光？──
啊！難不成
我們始終活在夢鄉！
這光景是多麼悲涼。

親愛的，我再也沒得好說，
但這份愛從未流逝，
懇切冬季刺戳五月的前胸，
它的猩紅玫瑰碎裂了冬霜，
暴風雨顛簸的船艦
將在某個海灣覓得避風港，
我們亦將覓得港灣。

除了再度親吻，離別，
再也沒得好說，
不，咱不該沉淪悔恨，
我有我的美，──你有你的藝術。
不，切莫再說，
一個世界，兩人不夠，
諸如你和我。

– **My Voice** –

Within this restless, hurried, modern world
We took our hearts' full pleasure—You and I,
And now the white sails of our ship are furled,
And spent the lading of our argosy.

Wherefore my cheeks before their time are wan,
For very weeping is my gladness fled,
Sorrow hath paled my lip's vermilion,
And Ruin draws the curtains of my bed.

But all this crowded life has been to thee
No more than lyre, or lute, or subtle spell
Of viols, or the music of the sea
That sleeps, a mimic echo, in the shell.

– 我的聲音 –

在這般倉皇匆促的世間
我們盡情享樂——你與我，
而今我將白帆收捲，
耗盡大船上的載貨。

為何我的面頰憔悴不逢時，
因每次悲泣，幸福亦飛逝，
傷懷蒼白了我唇的朱紅，
廢墟拉起我床畔的布簾。

然在這場變化多端的人生，
對你猶如豎琴，抑或詩琴，
或是維奧爾琴的迷離咒語，
或沉寐模擬貝殼回聲的海洋樂音。

– Γλυκοπικρο ερω –

Sweet, I blame you not, for mine the fault was, had I not been
made of common clay
I had climbed the higher heights unclimbed yet, seen the fuller air,
the larger day.

From the wildness of my wasted passion I had struck a better,
clearer song,
Lit some lighter light of freer freedom, battled with some Hydra-
headed wrong.

Had my lips been smitten into music by the kisses that but made
them bleed,
You had walked with Bice and the angels on that verdant and
enamelled meed.

I had trod the road which Dante treading saw the suns of seven
circles shine,
Ay! perchance had seen the heavens opening, as they opened to the
Florentine.

And the mighty nations would have crowned me, who am
crownless now and without name,
And some orient dawn had found me kneeling on the threshold of
the House of Fame.

- 親愛的（愛之花）-

親愛的，我並不怪你，是我的錯，若我不是凡塵俗人
就能攀爬那未登高處，眼底盡收遼闊風光，豐富時光。

我從殆盡的熱情荒野，彈奏出更優美清亮的曲調，
點燃更自由明耀的自由之光，與可惡九頭蛇搏鬥。

倘若將我被吻到滲血的唇，打擊成音樂，
你就能和貝緹麗彩與天使走在搪瓷般的蔥綠草原。

我已踏遍但丁漫步仰望七顆閃耀太陽的道路，
是的！天堂之門為翡冷翠人敞開時偶然可見。

強大國度可加冕我，如今摘冠無名的我，
東方旭日發現我跪在名譽殿堂的門檻前。

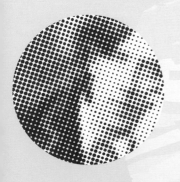

I had sat within that marble circle where the oldest bard is as the young,
And the pipe is ever dropping honey, and the lyre's strings are ever strung.

Keats had lifted up his hymeneal curls from out the poppy-seeded wine,
With ambrosial mouth had kissed my forehead, clasped the hand of noble love in mine.

And at springtide, when the apple-blossoms brush the burnished bosom of the dove,
Two young lovers lying in an orchard would have read the story of our love;

Would have read the legend of my passion, known the bitter secret of my heart,
Kissed as we have kissed, but never parted as we two are fated now to part.

For the crimson flower of our life is eaten by the cankerworm of truth,
And no hand can gather up the fallen withered petals of the rose of youth.

Yet I am not sorry that I loved you— ah! what else had I a boy to do?
For the hungry teeth of time devour, and the silent-footed years pursue.

我坐在大理石弧形劇場，老邁吟遊詩人一如青年，
笛子滲出蜜，豎琴弦彈奏，數年如一日。

濟慈自罌粟籽酒抬起頭，噘起他哼唱婚禮之歌的唇，
瓊漿玉液般的嘴親吻我額，情感高尚地輕拍我的手。

滿潮之際，蘋果花刷過白鴿的發亮胸膛，
躺在果園的年輕愛侶，已讀過我倆愛的故事。

讀過我的熱情傳奇，知曉我內心的苦澀祕密，
如過去般吻，即使當下注定分離，永不離別。

真相的尺蠖啃噬了我們人生的朱紅花蕊，
沒有一隻手能聚攏青春薔薇凋零的花瓣。

但我不後悔愛過你──啊！我這樣的男孩能怎麼做？
光陰飢餓的尖齒啃噬，悄然無聲的年歲緊追而至。

Rudderless, we drift athwart a tempest, and when once the storm of youth is past,
Without lyre, without lute or chorus, Death the silent pilot comes at last.

And within the grave there is no pleasure, for the blindworm battens on the root,
And Desire shudders into ashes, and the tree of Passion bears no fruit.

Ah! what else had I to do but love you? God's own mother was less dear to me,
And less dear the Cytheraean rising like an argent lily from the sea.

I have made my choice, have lived my poems, and, though youth is gone in wasted days,
I have found the lover's crown of myrtle better than the poet's crown of bays.

無舵漂泊轉向暴風雨，我們等待青春暴風過境之後，
沒有豎琴，沒有詩琴，沒有合唱，沉默死神舵手終於降臨。

墓裡無歡愉，啃著根部的無足蜥蜴肥碩，
欲望顫抖成了灰燼，熱情之樹不結果實。

啊！除了愛你，我還能怎麼做？對我，上帝之母不若你親，
而愛神猶如自海洋冉冉升起的銀白百合，也不曾這般親近。

我已經下好決定，活出我的詩歌，儘管青春荒廢逝去，
我卻發現，愛人的桃金孃冠，遠比詩人的月桂冠美麗。

〈黑色改編曲第三號：亨利・歐文先生扮演腓力二世〉
（Arrangement in Black, No.3: Sir Henry Irving as Philip II of Spain, 1876）
場景出自丁尼生劇作《瑪麗女王》。

沉默房裡，黑影沉重潛行，
死者飛快飄忽，大門開敞，
遭逢謀害的兄長地底高升，
鬼魂的死白手指擱在你肩，
在林地進行一場寂寞決鬥，
碎裂的劍，窒息的呼喊，千瘡百孔，
當一切結束，你復仇的炯炯雙瞳，——
都已足夠，——而你已成功。

更多威嚴創作登場！狂暴李爾王
在你一聲令下，跟尖聲訕笑的愚者
漫遊至石楠荒原，羅密歐，
你應引誘他愛上你。絕望恐懼
令理查三世拔出劍鞘的不忠匕首——
你為莎士比亞備好號角，並透過他唇吹奏！

– Fabien Dei Franchi: To My Friend – Henry Irving

The silent room, the heavy creeping shade,
The dead that travel fast, the opening door,
The murdered brother rising through the floor,
The ghost's white fingers on thy shoulders laid,

---

34 亨利‧歐文（Henry Irving, 1838-1905），英國名演員，出演過眾多莎士比亞名劇。

And then the lonely duel in the glade,
The broken swords, the stifled scream, the gore,
Thy grand revengeful eyes when all is o'er,—
These things are well enough,—but thou wert made

For more august creation! frenzied Lear
Should at thy bidding wander on the heath
With the shrill fool to mock him, Romeo
For thee should lure his love, and desperate fear
Pluck Richard's recreant dagger from its sheath—
Thou trumpet set for Shakespeare's lips to blow!

〈紫羅蘭與灰的變奏曲——第厄普市場〉

（Variations in violet and grey—Market Place, Dieppe, 1885）

– Serenade (for music) –

The western wind is blowing fair
Across the dark Aegean sea,
And at the secret marble stair
My Tyrian galley waits for thee.
Come down! the purple sail is spread,
The watchman sleeps within the town,
O leave thy lily-flowered bed,
O Lady mine come down, come down!

She will not come, I know her well,
Of lover's vows she hath no care,
And little good a man can tell
Of one so cruel and so fair.
True love is but a woman's toy,
They never know the lover's pain,
And I who loved as loves a boy
Must love in vain, must love in vain.

O noble pilot tell me true
Is that the sheen of golden hair?
Or is it but the tangled dew
That binds the passion-flowers there?
Good sailor come and tell me now
Is that my Lady's lily hand?
Or is it but the gleaming prow,
Or is it but the silver sand?

– 小夜曲（配樂）–

西風和煦吹送
在黝黑愛琴海，
祕密的大理石台階上
我的蒂爾艦隊等候你。
下來吧！紫色船帆已張，
城裡的守望者昏昏沉睡，
噢，離開你的百合花床，
噢，我的夫人，下來吧！

她不會來的，我懂她，
她不在意情人的誓言，
男人無法辨別
殘酷美麗的女子。
真愛不過是女人的玩物，
她們從不知情人的傷痛，
我的愛就如對男孩的愛
勢必無功而返，勢必愛得空白。

噢，高貴舵手，告訴我真相，
那可是金黃秀髮的光澤？
抑或不過是凝結露水
糾盤起那兒的西番蓮？
好水手，快請告訴我，
那豈是夫人的百合玉手？
抑或只是爍亮船首？
或是銀白沙灘？

No! no! 'tis not the tangled dew,
'Tis not the silver-fretted sand,
It is my own dear Lady true
With golden hair and lily hand!
O noble pilot steer for Troy,
Good sailor ply the labouring oar,
This is the Queen of life and joy
Whom we must bear from Grecian shore!

The waning sky grows faint and blue,
It wants an hour still of day,
Aboard! aboard! my gallant crew,
O Lady mine away! away!
O noble pilot steer for Troy,
Good sailor ply the labouring oar,
O loved as only loves a boy!
O loved for ever evermore!

不！不！那不是凝結露水，
不是海水啃噬的銀白沙灘，
真真實實是我親愛的夫人
金黃秀髮和猶如百合的手！
噢，高貴舵手航向特洛伊，
好水手來回搖著費力船槳，
她就是生命與喜悅的母后，
我們必須從希臘海岸帶回！

蒼蒼天空緩緩轉為微弱淡藍，
它渴望得到早晨的寧靜時刻，
上船！上船！我的英勇船員，
噢，我的夫人已走！已離去！
噢，高貴舵手航向特洛伊，
好水手來回搖著費力船槳，
噢，就如同對男孩的愛，
噢，永無止盡地被愛著。

〈藍與金的夜曲——老貝特西橋〉

(Nocturne: Blue and Gold—Old Battersea Bridge, 1872-7)

〈藍與銀的夜曲——契爾西〉

(Nocturne: Blue and Silver—Chelsea, 1871)

– Impression du Matin –

The Thames nocturne of blue and gold
Changed to a Harmony in grey:
A barge with ochre-coloured hay
Dropt from the wharf: and chill and cold

The yellow fog came creeping down
The bridges, till the houses' walls
Seemed changed to shadows, and S. Paul's
Loomed like a bubble o'er the town.

Then suddenly arose the clang
Of waking life; the streets were stirred
With country waggons: and a bird
Flew to the glistening roofs and sang.

But one pale woman all alone,
The daylight kissing her wan hair,
Loitered beneath the gas lamps' flare,
With lips of flame and heart of stone.

– 清晨印象 –

泰晤士河的藍金夜曲
褪為和聲般的灰：
駁船在碼頭卸下
赭黃乾草：刺骨冰寒

淡黃薄霧，躡手躡腳
攀過橋，一直到房舍的牆
似轉為陰影，聖保羅教堂
猶如氣泡，隱現凌駕城鎮。

剎那間，鏗鏘的聲響揚起，
驚醒深寐生命；鄉間馬車
街道騷動不已：一隻孤鳥
飛越閃耀屋頂啼啼。

但有名蒼白婦人獨守空閨，
日照光輝親吻她褪色的髮，
瓦斯燈閃閃光火之下流連，
唇如火焰般，心則若堅石。

– In the Gold Room: A Harmony –

Her ivory hands on the ivory keys
Strayed in a fitful fantasy,
Like the silver gleam when the poplar trees
Rustle their pale-leaves listlessly,
Or the drifting foam of a restless sea
When the waves show their teeth in the flying breeze.

Her gold hair fell on the wall of gold
Like the delicate gossamer tangles spun
On the burnished disk of the marigold,
Or the sunflower turning to meet the sun
When the gloom of the dark blue night is done,
And the spear of the lily is aureoled.

And her sweet red lips on these lips of mine
Burned like the ruby fire set
In the swinging lamp of a crimson shrine,
Or the bleeding wounds of the pomegranate,
Or the heart of the lotus drenched and wet
With the spilt-out blood of the rose-red wine.

– 黃金屋：和聲 –

她象牙白色的雙手，緊握住象牙白色的鑰匙，
迷失在斷續的幻想，
散發出銀色光輝，猶如白楊樹的蒼白樹葉
無精打采地沙沙作響，
抑或躁動大海上漂泊的泡沫
飄揚微風中，海浪露出利齒。

她的金黃髮絲落在金黃牆壁，
彷彿那糾纏結網的細膩蛛絲
旋繞在萬壽菊的爍亮花盤上，
或轉過臉迎接盛陽的太陽花，
深藍夜晚的陰鬱已不再，
月色光暈照耀百合嫩枝。

她的甜蜜紅唇壓上我的，
彷若紅寶石的焰火燃燒
在緋紅神龕的搖曳油燈，
或番石榴的滲血傷口，
抑或浸濕的蓮花之心，
玫瑰紅酒濺灑的鮮血。

〈藍與金的和聲：孔雀廳〉
（Harmony in Blue and Gold: The Peacock Room, 1876-77）
惠斯勒唯一的室內設計作品。原位於倫敦肯辛頓區，
收藏家弗利爾於 1904 年將整座房間買下，並搬至美國。孔雀廳現存於華盛頓特區的弗利爾藝廊。

– Impressions: Le Jardin –

The lily's withered chalice falls
Around its rod of dusty gold,
And from the beech-trees on the wold
The last wood-pigeon coos and calls.

The gaudy leonine sunflower
Hangs black and barren on its stalk,
And down the windy garden walk
The dead leaves scatter, - hour by hour.

Pale privet-petals white as milk
Are blown into a snowy mass:
The roses lie upon the grass
Like little shreds of crimson silk.

- 印象：花園 -

凋零百合花杯墜落
自霧金色的花桿邊，
最後一隻珠頸斑鳩
於高原的山毛櫸樹，呢噥呼喊。

向日葵花俏的獅鬃
黑黲荒蕪掛在花梗，
花園走道風兒吹送，
時時分分，枯槁葉片紛落。

蒼蒼水蠟樹花瓣如同乳奶白皙
吹送入風雪：
薔薇依偎著青草
彷如朱紅絲綢的細小碎片。

– Impressions: La Mer –

A white mist drifts across the shrouds,
A wild moon in this wintry sky
Gleams like an angry lion's eye
Out of a mane of tawny clouds.

The muffled steersman at the wheel
Is but a shadow in the gloom; —
And in the throbbing engine-room
Leap the long rods of polished steel.

The shattered storm has left its trace
Upon this huge and heaving dome,
For the thin threads of yellow foam
Float on the waves like ravelled lace.

〈海與雨〉(Sea and Rain, 1865)

– 印象：大海 –

雪白迷霧飄過幕罩，
風起雲湧的天空，狂亂的月
猶如怒獅透過牠的茶色鬃毛
洩露光火雙眼。

舵手遮蔽朦朧立於舵輪前
僅是昏暗之中一團黑影；——
在節奏震顫分明的引擎室
躍過悠長光亮的鋼鐵桿。

在這碩大起伏的穹蒼，
碎裂暴風遺留下痕跡，
黃色泡沫的纖細絲線
猶如纏結絲帶，隨浪浮沉。

Whistler

– Le Jardin des Tuileries –

This winter air is keen and cold,
And keen and cold this winter sun,
But round my chair the children run
Like little things of dancing gold.

Sometimes about the painted kiosk
The mimic soldiers strut and stride,
Sometimes the blue-eyed brigands hide
In the bleak tangles of the bosk.

And sometimes, while the old nurse cons
Her book, they steal across the square,
And launch their paper navies where
Huge Triton writhes in greenish bronze.

And now in mimic flight they flee,
And now they rush, a boisterous band—
And, tiny hand on tiny hand,
Climb up the black and leafless tree.

Ah! cruel tree! if I were you,
And children climbed me, for their sake
Though it be winter I would break
Into spring blossoms white and blue!

– 杜樂麗花園 –

今冬的空氣尖銳冷冽，
冬陽亦不失尖銳冷冽，
孩子在我的椅邊兜繞
彷若舞動的微小黃金。

偶然七彩報攤周圍
可見假士兵踢著英挺正步，
偶見藍眼盜賊躲藏
在那荒涼盤錯的小樹叢裡。

偶爾，老奶媽認真細讀
她手裡的書，他們鬼祟涉過廣場，
發動他們的紙作海軍隊，
龐大崔坦[35] 在綠油油的青銅上扭動。

他們這會兒假裝逃竄，
這下兒衝刺，喧鬧震耳的嬉戲——
然後，小手搭著小手，
爬上墨黑無葉的樹木。

啊！殘酷的樹！若我是你，
孩子爬上我身，為了他們，
即便冷冬，我願盛開綻放
那暖春的白藍花蕊！

---

35 希臘神話中的海之使者，亦是海王波塞頓之子。

– Fantaisies Décoratives: Le Panneau –

Under the rose-tree's dancing shade
There stands a little ivory girl,
Pulling the leaves of pink and pearl
With pale green nails of polished jade.

The red leaves fall upon the mould,
The white leaves flutter, one by one,
Down to a blue bowl where the sun,
Like a great dragon, writhes in gold.

The white leaves float upon the air,
The red leaves flutter idly down,
Some fall upon her yellow gown,
And some upon her raven hair.

She takes an amber lute and sings,
And as she sings a silver crane
Begins his scarlet neck to strain,
And flap his burnished metal wings.

She takes a lute of amber bright,
And from the thicket where he lies
Her lover, with his almond eyes,
Watches her movements in delight.

And now she gives a cry of fear,
And tiny tears begin to start:

- 唯美幻想：油畫 -

玫瑰樹的躍動樹影下方，
膚如象牙的小女孩駐足，
她摘下粉紅珍珠的葉片
以潔亮玉石般蒼鬱指甲。

嬌紅樹葉落在鬆軟土壤，
乳白葉片飄顫，一片接著一片，
墜落至靛藍的碗，太陽
猶如一頭巨龍，在金燦中扭曲。

白蒼蒼的葉片在空中漂浮，
紅殷殷的葉子了無生氣飄落，
有些落在她黃巴巴的袍上，
有些掉在她烏黑油亮的髮上。

她取出琥珀色的詩琴高歌，
歌唱時，一隻銀鶴
開始伸展他紅灼灼的頸子，
拍打亮澤光彩的金屬羽翼。

她取出那琥珀光澤的詩琴，
她生著杏眼的愛人
自他臥躺的灌木叢，
欣慰地凝視她的一舉一動。

這會兒她發出一聲驚恐嚎哭，
玉般淚珠傾巢而出：

荊棘尖刺扎傷了她
那浮著紅粉血管的貝殼玉耳。

而今她笑出歡樂的音符：
一片玫瑰花瓣凋落，
落在黃燦燦綢緞後
她浮著青筋的喉頸花朵。

以潔亮玉石般蒼鬱指甲，
她摘下粉紅珍珠的葉片，
膚如象牙的小女孩駐足
玫瑰樹的躍動樹影下方。

A thorn has wounded with its dart
The pink-veined sea-shell of her ear.

And now she laughs a merry note:
There has fallen a petal of the rose
Just where the yellow satin shows
The blue-veined flower of her throat.

With pale green nails of polished jade,
Pulling the leaves of pink and pearl,
There stands a little ivory girl
Under the rose-tree's dancing shade.

〈萊姆利吉斯的小玫瑰〉
（The Little Rose of Lyme Regis, 1895）
畫中女孩為當時萊姆利吉斯市長之女，蘿西・藍道（Rosie Randall）。

– Fantaisies Décoratives: Les Ballons –

Against these turbid turquoise skies
The light and luminous balloons
Dip and drift like satin moons
Drift like silken butterflies;

Reel with every windy gust,
Rise and reel like dancing girls,
Float like strange transparent pearls,
Fall and float like silver dust.

Now to the low leaves they cling,
Each with coy fantastic pose,
Each a petal of a rose
Straining at a gossamer string.

Then to the tall trees they climb,
Like thin globes of amethyst,
Wandering opals keeping tryst
With the rubies of the lime.

－ 唯美幻想：氣球 －

渾濁的綠松石天際
那輕盈光輝的氣球
緞般月亮下沉漂浮
彷若絲綢蝴蝶飄曳；

隨著陣陣狂風繾綣，
彷彿飛舞女孩旋繞，
猶如奇異透明珍珠漂浮，
一如銀色飛塵墜落沉浮。

它們如今緊挨著低垂的葉子，
一個個擺出忸怩的美妙身姿，
一個個皆玫瑰花瓣
竭力拉扯蜘蛛絲線。

它們攀上聳立的高木，
猶如淡薄的紫水晶球，
如同漂泊蛋白石守約
與椴樹的紅寶石聚首。

– Under the Balcony –

O beautiful star with the crimson mouth!
O moon with the brows of gold!
Rise up, rise up, from the odorous south!
And light for my love her way,
Lest her little feet should stray
On the windy hill and the wold!
O beautiful star with the crimson mouth!
O moon with the brows of gold!

O ship that shakes on the desolate sea!
O ship with the wet, white sail!
Put in, put in, to the port to me!
For my love and I would go
To the land where the daffodils blow
In the heart of a violet dale!
O ship that shakes on the desolate sea!
O ship with the wet, white sail!

O rapturous bird with the low, sweet note!
O bird that sits on the spray!
Sing on, sing on, from your soft brown throat!
And my love in her little bed
Will listen, and lift her head
From the pillow, and come my way!
O rapturous bird with the low, sweet note!
O bird that sits on the spray!

- 陽台下 -

噢，血盆大口的美麗星辰！
噢，端著黃金眉宇的月亮！
自芬芳的南方起身，來吧！
為我的愛人點亮方向，
以免她小小的腳迷失
在勁風吹拂的山丘與原野！
噢，血盆大口的美麗星辰！
噢，端著黃金眉宇的月亮！

噢，孤寂大海搖曳船隻！
噢，濕透揚起白帆的船！
為我進入海港，進港吧！
我與愛人即將前往
黃水仙搖曳的土地，
在紫羅蘭山谷之心！
噢，孤寂大海搖曳船隻！
噢，濕透揚起白帆的船！

噢，音符低沉甘美的痴狂鳥兒！
噢，乘在浪花上的鳥兒！
用柔軟褐色的喉嚨歌唱，唱吧！
我的愛人將在她的床畔
從她的枕頭上抬頭聆聽
並且前來找我！
噢，音符低沉甘美的痴狂鳥兒！
噢，乘在浪花上的鳥兒！

噢，懸在震顫空氣的花蕊！
噢，雪白雙唇的花蕊！
下來吧，讓我的愛人戴上！
猶如皇冠在她的髮上死去，
在她睡袍的皺褶逐漸死去，
你會進入她小小輕盈的心！
噢，懸在震顫空氣的花蕊！
噢，雪白雙唇的花蕊！

O blossom that hangs in the tremulous air!
O blossom with lips of snow!
Come down, come down, for my love to wear!
You will die on her head in a crown,
You will die in a fold of her gown,
To her little light heart you will go!
O blossom that hangs in the tremulous air!
O blossom with lips of snow!

〈肉色與綠的變奏曲：陽台〉
（Variations in Flesh Colour and Green: The Balcony, 1865）
惠斯勒用濃烈的東方元素描繪一場河邊陽台的茶宴。

〈紫與玫瑰：六字款青花瓷〉
（Purple and Rose: The Lange Leizen of the Six Marks, 1864）
模特兒手持印有「大清康熙年制」的標準六字款青花瓷。

– 獻給我妻：致上詩歌集 –

寫不出冠冕堂皇的詩
做為短抒情詩的前奏；
但我敢說，我能從詩人，
變成一首詩。

若在這片凋落花瓣中
你覺得其中一片美麗，
愛就會將那花瓣飄送
直到它落在你的髮上。

當冷風與寒冬
蕭瑟所有缺愛的土壤，
花瓣會喃喃花園絮語，
你會聽懂。

– To My Wife: With a Copy of My Poems –

I can write no stately proem
Λs a prelude to my lay;
From a poet to a poem
I would dare to say.

For if of these fallen petals
One to you seem fair,

Love will waft it till it settles
On your hair.

And when wind and winter harden
All the loveless land,
It will whisper of the garden,
You will understand.

-「石榴屋」詩集 -

去吧，小書，
去找他，以珍珠角製詩琴，
吟唱黃金女孩的皓白雙足：
要求他凝望
你的書頁：或許有所幫助，他將在書頁
發現黃金少女漫舞。

- With a Copy of "A House of Pomegranates" -

Go, little book,
To him who, on a lute with horns of pearl,
Sang of the white feet of the Golden Girl:
And bid him look
Into thy pages: it may hap that he
May find that golden maidens dance through thee.

– On the Sale by Auction of – Keats' Love Letters

These are the letters which Endymion wrote
To one he loved in secret and apart,
And now the brawlers of the auction-mart
Bargain and bid for each poor blotted note,
Aye! for each separate pulse of passion quote
The merchant's price! I think they love not art
Who break the crystal of a poet's heart,
That small and sickly eyes may glare or gloat.

Is it not said, that many years ago,
In a far Eastern town some soldiers ran
With torches through the midnight, and began
To wrangle for mean raiment, and to throw
Dice for the garments of a wretched man,
Not knowing the God's wonder, or his woe?

− 濟慈情書拍賣會 −

這些是恩底彌翁寫的書信
給他偷偷愛著，分隔兩地的愛人，
拍賣會上，人們爭先恐後
為了每個墨水字叫價競標，
是！每個熱情字句的脈動
皆是商人標價！我想他們不愛
打碎詩人心靈結晶的藝術，
狹小病態的眼珠怒瞪，貪婪注視。

可不是有個傳說？好多好多年前，
在遙遠東方城鎮，士兵們在夜半
高舉火炬奔竄，為了件
薄衣衫爭吵，擲骰子
爭奪一介可憐男人的衣裳，
卻不識上帝奇蹟，抑或他的悲哀。

– Symphony in Yellow –

An omnibus across the bridge
Crawls like a yellow butterfly,
And, here and there a passer-by
Shows like a little restless midge.

Big barges full of yellow hay
Are moored against the shadowy wharf,
And, like a yellow silken scarf,
The thick fog hangs along the quay.

The yellow leaves begin to fade
And flutter from the temple elms,
And at my feet the pale green Thames
Lies like a rod of rippled jade.

- 黃色交響曲 -

一輛公車跨越橋墩
彷彿鵝黃蝴蝶徐徐，
這兒那裡來了路人
庸庸碌碌猶如小蚊。

駁船滿載黃色稻草
停泊在陰霾碼頭邊，
猶如一條黃色絲巾，
濃霧懸掛在突堤邊。

杏黃葉片色澤漸褪
在神殿榆樹梢飄揚，
泰晤士河在我腳邊蒼翠
如漣漪翠玉的權杖躺仰。

〈沃平〉（Wapping, 1860-4）
沃平位於泰晤士河畔，曾是倫敦主要碼頭之一。

– In the Forest –

Out of the mid-wood's twilight
Into the meadow's dawn,
Ivory limbed and brown-eyed,
Flashes my Faun!

He skips through the copses singing,
And his shadow dances along,
And I know not which I should follow,
Shadow or song!

O Hunter, snare me his shadow!
O Nightingale, catch me his strain!
Else moonstruck with music and madness
I track him in vain!

－ 森林裡 －

森林中央，隱隱薄暮
縱躍入綠草黎明之間，
乳白四肢，褐黃雙眼，
我的牧神閃現！

哼著曲調，躍過灌木林，
陰影隨著他的舞步飄搖，
我不知道應當跟隨哪個，
是掠影，抑或歌聲！

噢，獵人，設圈套逮他的掠影！
噢，夜鶯，幫我捕捉他的旋律！
樂音及瘋癲令我迷濛狂亂
跟蹤最終無功而返！

國家圖書館出版品預行編目資料

我能從詩人，變成一首詩：王爾德詩選 . II /
王爾德（Oscar Wilde）著；
張家綺譯 . -- 初版 . -- 臺中市：好讀，2018.12
　　面；　公分 . --（典藏經典；118）

ISBN 978-986-178-476-2（平裝）
873.51　　　　　　　　　　　　　　107018471

好讀出版

典藏經典 118

我能從詩人，變成一首詩：王爾德詩選 II
Selected Poems of Oscar Wilde: II

填寫線上讀者回函
獲得更多好讀資訊

作　　者／王爾德 Oscar Wilde
繪　　者／詹姆斯．惠斯勒 James Abbott Whistler
譯　　者／張家綺
總 編 輯／鄧茵茵
文字編輯／王智群
美術編輯／廖勁智
行銷企畫／劉恩綺
發 行 所／好讀出版有限公司
　　　　　407 台中市西屯區工業 30 路 1 號
　　　　　407 台中市西屯區大有街 13 號（編輯部）
TEL: 04-23157795　FAX: 04-23144188　http://howdo.morningstar.com.tw
（如對本書編輯或內容有意見，請來電或上網告訴我們）
法律顧問／陳思成律師

總 經 銷／知己圖書股份有限公司
106 台北市大安區辛亥路一段 30 號 9 樓
TEL: 02-23672044 ／ 23672047　FAX: 02-23635741
407 台中市西屯區工業 30 路 1 號 1 樓
TEL: 04-23595819　FAX: 04-23595493
E-mail:service@morningstar.com.tw
網路書店：http://www.morningstar.com.tw
讀者專線：04-23595819#230
郵政劃撥：15060393（知己圖書股份有限公司）

印　　刷／上好印刷股份有限公司
初　　版／西元 2018 年 12 月 15 日
定　　價／ 200 元
如有破損或裝訂錯誤，請寄回台中市 407 西屯區工業 30 路 1 號更換（好讀倉儲部收）